THE
ULTIMATE
FOOTBALL
JOKE BOOK

CONTENTS

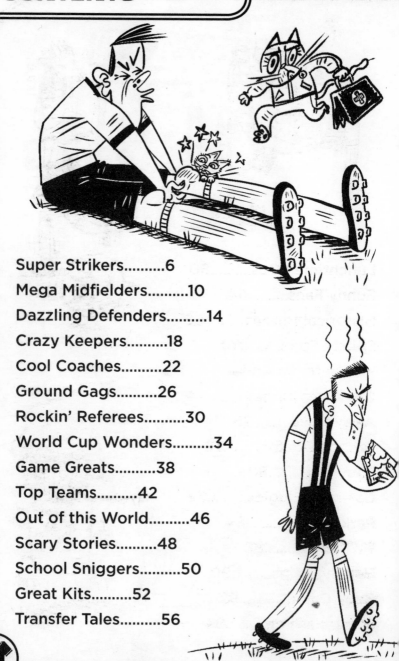

Super Strikers..........6
Mega Midfielders..........10
Dazzling Defenders..........14
Crazy Keepers..........18
Cool Coaches..........22
Ground Gags..........26
Rockin' Referees..........30
World Cup Wonders..........34
Game Greats..........38
Top Teams..........42
Out of this World..........46
Scary Stories..........48
School Sniggers..........50
Great Kits..........52
Transfer Tales..........56

Lunchtime LOLs..........60

Funny Fans..........64

Historical Heroes..........68

Sporty Stars..........70

International Action..........72

Creature Cringes..........74

Away Days..........76

Doctor, Doctor..........78

Film Fun..........80

Car-razy Giggles..........82

Park Pranks..........84

TV Times..........86

Gaming Gags..........90

Baby Games..........92

Footy Fashion..........94

Why doesn't Lionel Messi have any friends?

Because he's a Barce-loner.

What do you get if you cross Portugal's top striker with a sweet treat?

Cristiano Ronal-donut.

HAHA!

Which striker keeps returning to Arsenal?

Pierre-Emerick A-boomerang.

Why did the manager sign a porcupine to his squad?

It gave his team lots of points.

Which Egyptian star gobbles strawberries, apples, grapes and oranges?

Fruit Salah.

Which goalscorer loves to put the ball through a defender's legs?

Nutmeg-an Rapinoe

SUPER STRIKERS

Who is the slippiest striker?

Antoine Grease-mann.

HA!

Why couldn't the striker stop scratching himself?

Because he was Marcus Rash-ford.

What happens if you mix an England striker with strong winds?

You get a Hurry-Kane.

Which Liverpool star never says yes?

Roberto Firm no.

Which Brazil legend loves horses?

Neigh-mar.

Why do wingers write big 'X' signs on the grass?

Their job is to make crosses on the pitch.

What did the Spanish midfielder say when his teammate was upset?

What's the Mata with you?

Why was the player always cuddling his teammates?

He was a holding midfielder.

Why was the midfielder underground?

The boss told him to play in the hole.

11

MEGA MIDFIELDERS

Why do the best midfielders wear glasses and take dictionaries onto the pitch?

So that they read the game well.

Why did the winger stand by the gate?

Her manager told her to stay close to de-fence.

Why did the midfielder take a hosepipe to the game?

So he could spray passes.

What do you call a midfielder who keeps running during a game?

Miles.

Why was the pitch soaking wet?

Because the midfielders dribbled all over it.

What type of player always tidies up the pitch?

A sweeper.

Which centre-back do you find on a riverbed?

John Stones.

Who is the quickest defender?

Hurry Maguire.

Which England hero is easy to spot in the dark?

Millie Bright.

Why did the centre-back have a calculator in her pocket?

In case there was a count-er attack.

BAHAHA!

Why did the defender throw his watch in the bin just before the match finished?

He was wasting time.

Why does the defender always miss games?

Because he's left-back in the changing room.

Why did the defender not have a head, arms or upper body?

He was a centre-half.

What do you call a defender who collapses on the pitch?

A fall-back.

How do defenders get rid of mice in the kitchen?

They use the offside mouse trap.

What did one defensive wall say to the other?

Meet you at the corner.

Which defender always finishes third in competitions?

Lucy Bronze.

Why can't goalkeepers stop sneezing?

They always catch colds.

Which former US goalkeeper was awful saving one-on-ones?

Hope-less Solo.

A team was thrashing their opponents 10-0 so the goalkeeper had nothing to do. He started drilling for water. "Why are you doing that?" his teammate asked.

"This is well boring," he replied.

Which South American country has the most goalkeepers?

El Save-ador.

Why do goalkeepers have loads of money?

Because they're always saving.

19

What did the goalkeeper say to the ball as she threw it away?

Catch you later.

What's a goalkeeper's favourite snack?

Beans on post.

What happened when two keepers went on holiday together?

They had a glove-ly time.

A goalkeeper invited his team over for dinner. He put a cloth on the table and told the players not to drop any food on it.

He really wanted to keep a clean sheet.

What do you call a player who stands behind the goalkeeper?

Annette.

Goalkeeping coach: "I'll phone you later to talk about the next game. What's your number?"

Goalkeeper: "1".

COOL COACHES

Why did the nose stop playing for his footy team?

The coach wasn't picking him.

What do managers and triangles have in common?

They always need three points.

Why did the manager always bring a ladder to matches?

She wanted to get higher in the league.

Pep Guardiola told Sergio Aguero to take cardboard to the game.

He wanted him to get in the box.

COOL COACHES

The lights went out in Chelsea's dressing room.

The players could still see because they had Lamps.

What did the Liverpool manager do when his bike went missing?

He called the Klopps.

Why couldn't the manager run very fast?

Because he was a slow coach.

Why don't Australian marsupials become coaches?

They don't have the koala-fications.

In training one day, the coach took the defenders to a playground. "Why are we here, boss?" asked one of the defenders.

"You need to practise slide tackles," she replied.

Why does Aston Villa's ground always have excitement and drama?

Because it's Thriller Park.

Why are Manchester United players always freezing?

They play at Cold Trafford.

How did the groundsman keep players off the pitch?

He turfed them out.

Where do stinging insects play football?

Wem-bee-ly Stadium.

BAHAHA!

GROUND GAGS

Which Premier League stadium never gets old?

Moli-new.

Which ground has a deep end and a shallow end?

Liver-pool.

Where does a parent take their well-behaved child to watch football?

Good-son Park.

Which club's ground is built with millions of screws and nuts?

Bolt-on Wanderers.

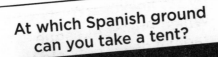
At which Spanish ground can you take a tent?

The Nou Camp.

How does a referee leave a football stadium?

Through the bye-bye line.

HA!

Why did the linesman never have any energy?

He was always flagging on the side of the pitch.

Which striker do refs love?

Jamie VAR-dy.

What did the South American ref say to a diving player?

I don't Bolivia.

ROCKIN' REFEREES

Player: This referee is an author as well!

Captain: Why do you think that?

Player: He says I'm going in his book.

The referee told the player he could take the free-kick when the ball was stationary.

So he swapped it for a pencil.

The players complained to the referee about a giant hole in the middle of the pitch.

The referee said she'll look into it.

Why could the World Cup's top scorer no longer lift his legs?

He was wearing golden boots.

HA!

Which World Cup finalist loves playing hide-and-seek with his teammates?

Look-here Modric.

Which legendary winner celebrated with a takeaway?

Diego Mara-doner kebab.

Which German World Cup winner kept setting off the fire warning system?

Philipp Lahm-bell.

Which England hero sells cheese, cooked meat, pasta and salad?

Deli Alli.

WORLD CUP WONDERS

When was the last time France won the World Cup?

At full-time when the whistle was blown, of course.

What type of songs will be played at the 2022 World Cup?

Qatar music.

Why did the 2018 World Cup go so quickly?

The games were all played in a Russia.

Which Brazilian World Cup star loves oranges and bananas?

Peel-é.

Who do you get if you cross a Chelsea legend with a scary spider?

John Terry-antula.

Why do French fans try to touch Kylian Mbappe's foot?

Because he's a leg-end for his country.

How did the legendary Chelsea and Arsenal keeper pay for his shopping?

At the Cěch-out.

Which Man United hero got a job as an airline pilot?

Flyin' Giggs.

Even though Griezmann triumphed in the final, he never stops complaining ...

Because he's a World Cup whiner.

GAME GREATS

Why did Rooney take an umbrella to the game?

In case it Wayned.

Which England ace never doubted he would score?

Jermaine Defoe-nitely.

Which Chelsea favourite always barked orders on the pitch?

Didier Dog-ba.

Which famous giant striker always hit his head on the crossbar?

Peter Ouch!

Where's a footballer's fave place to sunbathe and swim?

Chel-sea.

Which Spanish ground has extra fire extinguishers installed?

The Burn-abéu.

What happens if you cross a famous Portuguese club with a London landmark?

Big Benfica.

Which team weighs the most?

Ever-tonne.

43

The Real Madrid captain was asked if he liked the team's new kit.

"It's all white I suppose," he replied.

HA!

Which club loves riding horses?

PS Gee-gee.

Which team takes the train to away matches?

Locomotive Moscow.

BAHAHA!

Why was the French team not worried about defeats?

Because they had nothing Tou-lose.

OUT OF THIS WORLD

Why do astronauts make great midfielders?

They are always looking for space.

Why do players turn green and fly spaceships if a match goes beyond 90 minutes?

Because it's extra-terrestrial time.

Why is an empty stadium just like outer space?

Because it has no atmosphere.

BAHAHA!

Why do rocket scientists make good strikers?

They blast the ball.

How do astronauts organise
a footy match in space?

They planet.

Why do ghosts not take a shower after a game?

It dampens their spirits.

BAHAHA!

Which team do volcanoes support?

Lava-pool.

What's a pirate's favourite team?

Arrrrrrrrr-senal.

HAHA!

The zombie worked hard to become a professional footballer.

He was very dead-icated.

49

Why was the footballer still at school during half-term?

He was waiting for the half-term whistle.

The teacher didn't like having an Argentine hero at school.

He made her classroom Messi.

Why did the P.E. teacher ask the kids to bring pencils and paper to training?

He was hoping for a draw.

What happened when the teacher tied a team's bootlaces together?

They all went on a school trip.

BAHAHA!

Why are Manchester City midfielders good at maths?

They always make quick one-twos.

The players went to the store to look for a kit with a camouflage design.

They couldn't see anything they liked.

BAHAHA!

Why did the prison footy team never wear warm layers in winter?

They hated being under a vest.

What do you call the manager who wears expensive, stylish suits?

The Hugo Boss.

Why don't footballers play in ballet clothes?

They are tutu difficult to get on.

Why was the number 6 shirt afraid of the number 7 shirt?

Because seven ate nine.

What do you call a footballer wearing only one boot?

Eileen.

BAHAHA!

Why did the footballers wear black and yellow stripes?

Because they were the B team.

LOL!

Where do American managers get their team kits from?

New Jersey.

Why was the team sent too many tiny football shirts?

They accidentally ordered XS kit.

TRANSFER TALES

A player turned down a move to Italy.

He didn't know the way Inter Milan.

Which player will a manager never buy?

Owen Goal.

BAHAHA!

The manager was looking to sign someone to unlock defences.

He needed a key player.

Which window is only open in the summer and January?

The transfer window.

A player was desperate to transfer to a team in the south of France.

He wanted to have a Nice time.

Why did the burglar hurt his fingers?

Because the transfer window suddenly closed.

Why did the club chairman go shopping at the mask factory?

He was looking to buy some new faces.

Manchester United needed someone with experience who could also look after animals.

They were after a vet-eran player.

Why did Chelsea have a labrador, spaniel and poodle in their team?

Because of the transfer em-bark-go.

HA!

How did the manager sign Father Christmas without paying any money?

He had a free transfer Claus.

LUNCHTIME LOLs

What spice do defenders hate?

Nutmeg.

What is Sergio Aguero's favourite sandwich?

Argen-tuna and mayonnaise.

What's a footballer's favourite hot drink?

Penal-tea.

What do East London footy fans have with their fries?

A West Hamburger.

Why do Norwich City love vegetables?

They play at Carrot Road.

Why wouldn't the Mexico team chat about their match during dinner?

They didn't want to taco 'bout it.

In pre-season training, the squad all had dry throats.

The physio gave them a thirst-aid kit.

Why do footballers eat oranges at half-time?

It makes them peel better.

FUNNY FANS

Why do Chelsea fans always look upset?

Because they've got The Blues.

What's black and white and bounces?

Newcastle fans on a trampoline.

HAHA!

What's black and white, bounces and then groans?

Newcastle fans falling off a trampoline.

BAHAHA!

Where do footy-crazy babies sleep?

In a mas-cot.

FUNNY FANS

What's the name of the funniest footy fan?

Owen Lee Joe King.

Which English team has the most fans?

Sup-portsmouth.

Two football fans watch their team in action every Saturday, but they think the defence isn't strong enough.

They thought they were playing weakly.

Who is the most famous supporter in Germany?

Brian Munich.

Why was the Anglo-Saxon king fed up with football?

His team just Canute win a game.

Which Second World War hero never saw his team lose?

Win-ston Churchill.

Where do royalty watch football?

At Crystal Palace.

How did the explorer get to the game?

She took the Christopher Colum-bus.

Two footballers play golf together on a day off. One of them takes two pairs of underwear. "Why have you got extra pants?" asks the player.

"In case I get a hole in one."

Usain Bolt quit sprinting to become a football player.

His team only won runner-up medals.

The manager decided to swap his striker for a bundle of rowing equipment.

It was a big oar deal.

What does a javelin thrower and the league's bottom team have in common?

They both chuck points away.

Why are tennis supporters noisier than football supporters?

Because they make more of a racquet.

What's the difference between San Marino and a teabag?

A teabag stays in the cup longer.

Why wasn't the Scotland team allowed to own a dog?

Because they couldn't hold on to a lead.

Coming home after the World Cup, the England team's luggage went missing at Heathrow.

They sued the airport but eventually lost their case.

At an international event, players could only take part if they were under five foot tall.

It was a mini tournament.

Why are the Hegerberg sisters such good players?

Because there's Nor-way to beat them.

England play Iceland at the weekend. Then next Tuesday they play Sainsbury's, before a tricky game away at ASDA.

CREATURE CRINGES

Why can't you play footy in the African grasslands?

There are too many cheetahs.

What football boots does a grizzly wear?

They don't wear boots – they go bear feet.

Why did the manager play a gull between the posts?

Because it was his tern to go in goal.

Which scaly creature stars for Real Madrid and Belgium?

Eden Lizard.

Why is the centipede always late for kick-off?

It takes him ages to put his boots on.

Why did the fan pack suntan lotion for an away game?

He was going to Sun-derland's Stadium of Light.

How long does it take to get to Newcastle?

A long Tyne.

When Tottenham built their new stadium, they decided to seat away fans right at the top of a high stand and charge them extra.

Visiting supporters said prices had gone through the roof.

DOCTOR, DOCTOR

Goalkeeper: "I've been dropped from the team because I can't hold the ball."

Doctor: "Don't worry. What you have is not catching."

Why was the player jumping around on one leg?

Because the doctor gave him a hop-operation.

Player: "Doctor, my team-mates say I'm a liar."

Doctor: "I find that very hard to believe."

Why did a cat become the footy team's doctor?

Because it had a first aid kit-ten.

Why did the coach need urgent medical help?

Because the game went to sudden death penalties.

Why do Star Wars fans like to play out wide?

Because they're good on the X-Wing.

HA!

Why do Juventus fans like watching old movies?

Because they're black and white.

What happened when the bear, panther, tiger and python played?

The referee Jungle Booked them.

Why couldn't Elsa and Anna play football?

Because the pitch was Frozen.

CAR-RAZY GIGGLES

Why did the footballer think sleeping under his car meant he wouldn't be late for the match?

Because he would wake up oily.

How does a spaceship pay for parking at Wembley Stadium?

At the parking meteor.

Why wasn't the car allowed to play football?

Because it only had one boot.

Which footballer will only buy a Fiesta, Mondeo or Focus?

Jordan Pick-Ford.

Why did the referee tell players to stay away from the slide?

Because of the off-slide rule.

HA!

Why do footy fans play on the swing after a victory?

They always swing when they're winning.

What does a seesaw and Norwich City have in common?

They both go down and back up a lot.

The team at the top of the table wouldn't visit the adventure playground.

They were worried about sliding down the league.

TV TIMES

A team's two strikers each scored a hat-trick in a game, without conceding.

They watched the goals on the 6-O'clock news.

The Premier League wants to create a pitch in the clouds.

All games will be shown on Sky Sports.

Why did the fan put his TV on top of a lamppost?

Because he wanted to watch the high-lights.

Which TV station only wants to show the dull 0-0 draws?

Channel bore.

HEE-HEE!

Which programme does the team at the bottom of the league, with no wins or draws all season, watch?

Pointless.

Who is the best footballer at the BBC?

iPlayer.

How does watching football on a screen make you feel better?

If it's on a tablet.

HAHA!

What do you get if you cross an ex-England striker with a lazy fan who watches TV all day?

A Crouch potato.

GAMING GAGS

Which console do the French team play FIFA on?

Nintendo Oui.

BAHAHA!

How do you get the Pikachu FC players back onto the team bus?

You poke 'em on.

Which striker dresses in red and blue, bounces around and pretends to be a plumber?

Super Mario Balotelli.

The PC had a virus called 'bad goalkeeper'.

It couldn't save anything.

How do babies beat defenders?

They use a dummy.

Where do three-year-olds learn to play football?

At Toddler Hotspur.

What's the youngest team in South America?

Boca Juniors.

BAHAHA!

Where are footy-mad babies taken to at 3pm on a Saturday?

To West Pram United.

LOL!

What do you call a very young footballer who just rests in the middle of the pitch and doesn't move?

A baby sitter.

FOOTY FASHION

What did the hat say to the footy scarf?

You hang around and I'll go on ahead.

How much is the kitman paid for ironing a footballer's clothes?

Not much, it's a flat rate but he gets paid in-creases.

A truck carrying Real Madrid t-shirts crashed on the motorway.

There were no casual-tees involved.

Knock-knock.

Who's there?

Tyrone.

Tyrone who?

Tyrone boot laces for once!